Draw or stick a picture
of your mummy here.

My Mummy

LADYBIRD BOOKS

UK | USA | Canada | Ireland | Australia | India | New Zealand | South Africa

Ladybird Books is part of the Penguin Random House group of companies
whose addresses can be found at global.penguinrandomhouse.com.

www.penguin.co.uk   www.puffin.co.uk   www.ladybird.co.uk

 Penguin
Random House
UK

First published 2018
003

Printed in China

A CIP catalogue record for this book is available from the British Library

ISBN: 978–0–241–32150–8

All correspondence to:
Ladybird Books
Penguin Random House Children's
80 Strand, London WC2R 0RL

It was **very** early in the morning and Peppa and George had woken up Daddy Pig and dragged him to the kitchen.
"We want to make Mummy a surprise breakfast!" said Peppa, excitedly.

"Arrhhhh," yawned Daddy Pig.
"Well, I **am** an expert at making pancakes."
"Yippee!" cheered Peppa. "Mummy loves pancakes."

Upstairs, Mummy Pig was in bed.
She could hear lots of noise.
BANG! CRASH!
"Hee! Hee! Hee! OOPS!"
"MUMMY!" shouted Peppa.
"We need you, Mummy!"

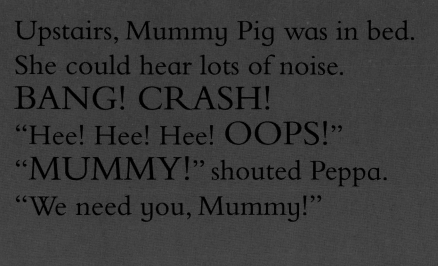

Mummy Pig got
out of bed and
went downstairs.

"We're making you a surprise breakfast, Mummy," explained Peppa. "But it went a bit wrong."

"Surprise!" mumbled Daddy Pig.
"How lovely," said Mummy Pig, smiling.

"Why don't you tidy up the mess?" said Mummy Pig.
"And I'll finish the breakfast."

Mummy Pig tossed the pancakes high up into the air and straight on to everyone's plates.

"Wow, Mummy!" Peppa and George cheered.
"You're amazing!"
"And these are delicious," added Daddy Pig, tucking in.

After breakfast, Peppa whispered to Daddy Pig, "Let's take Mummy to the beach."

"Great idea, Peppa," whispered Daddy Pig. "It is her favourite."

"Mummy!" cried Peppa. "We're taking you on a surprise trip!"

"How lovely," replied Mummy Pig. "I'll just get my things."

Mummy packed her bag,
then everyone hopped in the car.
"Let's go!" cheered Peppa.

"Oh, how lovely," said Mummy Pig, stepping
out of the car. "The beach . . . in the snow!"
"Oh," sighed Peppa. "It's **very** cold."

"Not to worry," said Mummy Pig. She pulled out nice, warm clothes for everyone, and then a table, some chairs and lots of toys. "Thank you, Mummy," said Peppa.

Peppa built a snow-castle, while
George and Daddy Pig played catch.
"You relax, Mummy," said Daddy Pig.
"George! Catch!"
The ball flew through the air
and was about to land on
Peppa's snow-castle . . .

"MUMMY!" shouted Peppa.
"We need you, Mummy!"

Mummy Pig jumped up and caught the ball just in time.

Ooooh!

"Wow, Mummy!"
gasped Peppa. "You're brilliant!"

"How about we have a nice lunch?" suggested Daddy Pig, getting the picnic things out. But, just as everyone was about to eat, there was a great gust of wind.

WHOOSH!

The food was whipped off the table and up into the air.

"MUMMY!" cried Peppa. "We need you, Mummy!"

Mummy Pig grabbed the umbrella and used it to catch all the picnic food!

"Wow, Mummy!" gasped Peppa. "You're so clever."

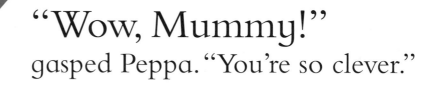

"Let's throw snowballs into the sea!"
said Peppa after they had eaten.
So Daddy Pig, Peppa and George
headed off to the sea, while Mummy Pig
read her book.

Daddy Pig and Peppa
had lots of fun.

But, when it was George's turn, he accidentally threw
Mr Dinosaur into the sea instead!
"Wahhhhh!" sobbed George, watching his dinosaur float away.
"MUMMY!" cried Peppa. "We need you, Mummy!"

Plonk!
Splash!

Mummy Pig ran towards the water's edge.
She saw Mr Dinosaur, pulled off her coat
and dived into the cold sea to get him!
"Ooooh!" she gasped.
"It is a little chilly."

She swam over to Mr Dinosaur, then picked
him up and swam quickly back to shore.
"Dine-saw, grrrr!" growled George, happily.
"Wow, Mummy!" said Peppa.
"You're SO brave."

Peppa, George and Daddy Pig
dried Mummy Pig with towels,
and soon she was nice and warm.
"I think it's time to head home,"
said Daddy Pig.
"Good idea," agreed
Mummy Pig, packing
up their things.

"*Goodbye, snowy beach!*" sang Peppa
all the way home.

After dinner, Mummy and Daddy Pig helped Peppa
and George get ready for bed. Then they tucked them
in with a story.
"Goodnight, Peppa. Goodnight, George," said Mummy Pig.
"Goodnight, bestest mummy in the whole world!"
giggled Peppa.

Mummy and Daddy Pig headed downstairs.
But, just as they sat down, they heard Peppa shout,
"MUMMY! We need you, Mummy!"

So Mummy Pig went back upstairs . . .

"Yes, Peppa?"
"I love you, Mummy!"
said Peppa, giving Mummy Pig
a great big hug.
"Wuv oo, Mummy-ig," said
George, and he gave her a
great big hug, too.

"I love you both," said
Mummy Pig. "Very much.
Now, goodnight, and I'll see
you in the morning."

"This is for you," said Daddy Pig,
giving Mummy Pig a present.

Mummy Pig opened it to find a great big bar of chocolate inside.
"Ooooh, thank you," she said, delighted.
Then she unwrapped the bar and saw . . .

. . . that **someone** had already had a little nibble!
"Daddy Pig!" she said, smiling.
 Daddy Pig looked very guilty and went bright red.
"I love you, Mummy Pig!"